This book
belongs to:

_____

_____

From:

_____

_____

Lola Dutch
I Love You So Much

KENNETH
AND SARAH JANE WRIGHT

BLOOMSBURY
CHILDREN'S BOOKS
NEW YORK LONDON OXFORD NEW DELHI SYDNEY

This is Lola. Lola Dutch.

Lola Dutch loves her friends SO MUCH.
Even when her friends have a case of . . .

. . . the grumps.
Gator was cranky and cold.
Crane couldn't find her favorite book.
And Pig was positively peevish.

"This is no way to start the day! I know just what to do," said Lola.

Gator needed to feel comfy and cozy.

Lola picked the fabric,

planned the pattern,

sewed up all the seams,

and by lunchtime she had a snuggly gift for Gator . . .

Gator was giddy.

"Gator, I love you so much," said Lola Dutch.

"Bear, have you seen Crane?"

"I think she's still looking for her book," said Bear. "She's quite upset."

"But her books are absolutely EVERYWHERE! I know just how to help," said Lola. "Gator, let's go!"

So, Gator gathered the books,

and Lola made a
peaceful nook . . .

while Pig trailed behind.

"Crane, I love you so much!" said Lola Dutch.

"Poor Pig. Do you feel left out?"
asked Lola. "I know just what you need.
Friends, to the park!"

Gator gathered Pig's favorite snacks.

Crane packed the kites.

Lola loaded the wagon.

And everyone was happy . . .

. . . until it started to rain.

"OH, NO!" said Lola. "Now the park is nothing but soggy puddles." Lola looked at Gator. Lola looked at Crane. Lola looked at Pig. "Wait . . . puddles?" said Lola.

puddles!

Bear met them at the door with fluffy towels and cocoa.
"Bear," said Lola, "today turned out to be the best EVER!
I made Gator cozy pajamas, built a reading spot for Crane, and
we took Pig to the park. No one has the grumps anymore!"

"You must love your friends so much," said Bear.

But then Lola realized she'd forgotten someone.
"Excuse me, Bear. I need to do one more thing!" said Lola.

How can I show Bear I love him so much? Lola wondered.

Maybe I could paint a picture?

Write a song?

Pick a bouquet of flowers?

Start a Bear fan club?

But it was just NOT ENOUGH!

"Oh, dear! What's the matter, Lola?" Bear asked.

"Bear, I'm trying to think of the perfect gift to show how much I love you, but I don't know what you love the MOST."

"This was all for me? Thank you," said Bear. "Well, if you *really* want to know what I love the most, it's . . ."

Lola Dutch.

"And I'm not the only one. Lola, you are such a
good friend to everyone, we wanted to do something
special for you, too. Come on, friends!"

Lola Dutch, we love

"You are all such wonderful
friends," said Lola.

"I don't think any of us can have the grumps for long,
because we have each other."

For Robyn & Jeff,
who, come what may, choose love

BLOOMSBURY CHILDREN'S BOOKS
Bloomsbury Publishing Inc., part of Bloomsbury Publishing Plc
1385 Broadway, New York, NY 10018

BLOOMSBURY, BLOOMSBURY CHILDREN'S BOOKS, and the Diana logo
are trademarks of Bloomsbury Publishing Plc

First published in the United States of America in December 2019 by Bloomsbury Children's Books

Bloomsbury books may be purchased for business or promotional use. For information on bulk purchases
please contact Macmillan Corporate and Premium Sales Department at specialmarkets@macmillan.com

Library of Congress Cataloging-in-Publication Data
Names: Wright, Kenneth, author. | Wright, Sarah Jane, illustrator.
Title: Lola Dutch I love you so much / by Kenneth Wright ; illustrated by Sarah Jane Wright.
Description: New York : Bloomsbury, 2019.
Summary: Lola Dutch loves all of her animal friends, so when three of them are
having a bad day she sets out to help them feel better.
Identifiers: LCCN 2019004269 (print) • LCCN 2019007564 (e-book)
ISBN 978-1-5476-0117-2 (hardcover) • ISBN 978-1-5476-0118-9 (e-book) • ISBN 978-1-5476-0119-6 (e-PDF)
Subjects: | CYAC: Friendship–Fiction. | Animals–Fiction. | Creative ability–Fiction. |
Mood (Psychology)–Fiction.
Classification: LCC PZ7.1.W79 Lp 2019 (print) | LCC PZ7.1.W79 (e-book) | DDC [E]–dc23
LC record available at https://lccn.loc.gov/2019004269

Art created with pencil, gouache, and watercolor
Typeset in Bodoni Six ITC Std • Book design by Jeanette Levy
Printed in China by Leo Paper Products, Heshan, Guangdong
2 4 6 8 10 9 7 5 3 1

All papers used by Bloomsbury Publishing Plc are natural, recyclable products
made from wood grown in well-managed forests. The manufacturing processes conform to the
environmental regulations of the country of origin.

To find out more about our authors and books visit www.bloomsbury.com and sign up for our newsletters.

Lola Dutch, I Love You So Much is a story about showing friends how much you care
for them. It's inspired in part by Gary Chapman's theory of the five love languages,
which says there are five ways people express and feel love from others: through words
of affirmation, acts of service, receiving gifts, quality time, and physical touch. Lola
knows Gator feels loved when she gives him a gift, Crane feels cared for when Lola
takes care of her, Pig wants quality time to feel loved, and Bear's touch, like a big hug,
is how he shares love. And for Lola, hearing her friends say "I
love you so much" and thanking her for being a good friend is
all the love she needs. What are the ways you feel loved? And
how can you show your friends you love them?

TEAM BEAR